AF228904

Thinking Critically: Abortion Rights

Naomi Rockler

San Diego, CA

For more information, contact:
ReferencePoint Press, Inc.
PO Box 27779
San Diego, CA 92198
www.ReferencePointPress.com

LIBRARY OF CONGRESS CATALOGING-IN-PUBLICATION DATA

Names: Rockler, Naomi, author.
Title: Thinking critically : abortion rights / by Naomi Rockler.
Other titles: Abortion rights
Description: San Diego, CA : ReferencePoint Press, Inc., 2025. | Series:
    Thinking critically | Includes bibliographical references and index.
Identifiers: LCCN 2024003984 (print) | LCCN 2024003985 (ebook) | ISBN
    9781678208448 (library binding) | ISBN 9781678208455 (ebook)
Subjects: LCSH: Abortion--Juvenile literature. | Reproductive
    rights--Juvenile literature.
Classification: LCC HQ767 .R635 2025 (print) | LCC HQ767 (ebook) | DDC
    342.08/4--dc23/eng/20240314
LC record available at https://lccn.loc.gov/2024003984
LC ebook record available at https://lccn.loc.gov/2024003985

Contents

"Literacy is the most basic currency of the knowledge economy we're living in today." Barack Obama (at the time a senator from Illinois) spoke these words during a 2005 speech before the American Library Association. One question raised by this statement is: What does it mean to be a literate person in the twenty-first century?

E.D. Hirsch Jr., author of *Cultural Literacy: What Every American Needs to Know*, answers the question this way: "To be culturally literate is to possess the basic information needed to thrive in the modern world. The breadth of the information is great, extending over the major domains of human activity from sports to science."

But literacy in the twenty-first century goes beyond the accumulation of knowledge gained through study and experience and expanded over time. Now more than ever literacy requires the ability to sift through and evaluate vast amounts of information and, as the authors of the Common Core State Standards state, to "demonstrate the cogent reasoning and use of evidence that is essential to both private deliberation and responsible citizenship in a democratic republic."

The Thinking Critically series challenges students to become discerning readers, to think independently, and to engage and develop their skills as critical thinkers. Through a narrative-driven, pro/con format, the series introduces students to the complex issues that dominate public discourse—topics such as gun control and violence, social networking, and medical marijuana. All chapters revolve around a single, pointed question such as Can Stronger Gun Control Measures Prevent Mass Shootings?, or Does Social Networking Benefit Society?, or Should Medical Marijuana Be Legalized? This inquiry-based approach introduces student researchers to core issues and concerns on a given topic. Each chapter includes one part that argues the affirmative and one part that argues the negative—all written by a single author. With the single-author format the predominant arguments for and against an issue can be synthesized into clear, accessible discussions supported by details and evidence including relevant facts, direct quotes, current examples, and statistical illustrations. All volumes include focus questions to guide students as they read each pro/con discussion, a list of key facts, and an annotated list of related organizations and websites for conducting further research.

The authors of the Common Core State Standards have set out the particular qualities that a literate person in the twenty-first century must have. These include the ability to think independently, establish a base of knowledge across a wide range of subjects, engage in open-minded but discerning reading and listening, know how to use and evaluate evidence, and appreciate and understand diverse perspectives. The new Thinking Critically series supports these goals by providing a solid introduction to the study of pro/con issues.

Abortion Rights

In September 2021 Texas implemented the Heartbeat Act. This law banned abortions when an embryo's heartbeat is detectable, which is around the sixth week of pregnancy. At the time this was the most restrictive abortion law in the United States, and it had a significant impact on seventeen-year-old Brooke Alexander from Corpus Christi, Texas.

Things had been looking up for Alexander, a high school drop-out from an abusive family. She was excited about her community college real estate classes and her new boyfriend, Billy High, whom she had met at a skateboard park. Then, two days before the Texas Heartbeat Act went into effect, Alexander discovered she was pregnant. She wanted to get an abortion. However, the local clinics had no openings due to the surge of women seeking abortions before the ban went into effect.

Instead, Alexander made an appointment at a pregnancy crisis center. She did not know that the main purpose of that center was to talk pregnant women and girls out of getting abortions. At the center, she had an ultrasound and learned she was pregnant with twins. Alexander considered traveling to another state for an abortion—or trying to, since she did not have the money to travel. But the people at the pregnancy center persuaded her not to terminate the pregnancy.

Alexander gave birth to twins Olivia and Kendall in April 2022, and she and High got married a few weeks later. The family moved to Florida after Billy joined the US Air Force. Instead of becoming a real estate agent, Brooke stayed home and struggled to care for the twins without the support of family and friends. She and Billy fought often.

A year later, at nineteen, Brooke expressed mixed feelings about how the Texas Heartbeat Act had impacted her life. On the one hand, she felt her life was much harder because of it. She missed her freedom and believed that parenthood was the only thing keeping her and Billy together. On the other hand, she loved Olivia and Kendall fiercely. "Who's to say what I would have done if the law wasn't in effect?" she says. "I don't want to think about it."[1]

Many pregnant women and girls like Brooke believe they should have the legal right to end an unwanted pregnancy without interference from legislators. Others insist that abortion should be illegal—or else legal only under specific, restrictive circumstances—because an unborn child is a living being. This conflict of beliefs is at the root of the abortion rights debate, one of the most polarizing debates in America today.

—Brooke Alexander High, a mother impacted by the Texas Heartbeat Law

What Is an Abortion?

An abortion is a medical procedure that ends a pregnancy. According to Planned Parenthood, a women's health organization that offers abortion services, about one in four women in the United States will have an abortion by the time they are forty-five years old. The Guttmacher Institute, a research organization that tracks abortion data, reports that there were approximately 930,000 abortions performed in the United States in 2020.

According to the Guttmacher Institute, about 80 percent of abortions are performed during the first nine weeks of pregnancy, and 93 percent are performed within the first thirteen weeks. (Pregnancies typically last about forty weeks.) Fewer than 1 percent of abortions are performed after a fetus is viable, which means that the fetus can possibly survive outside the uterus. This happens around twenty-two to twenty-four weeks. Abortions this late in a pregnancy are almost always performed in extreme cases only, like when the mother is likely to die if the pregnancy continues.

Most abortions are obtained by women in their twenties (57 percent), followed by those in their thirties (30 percent), teenagers (9 percent), and women forty and over (4 percent). A disproportionate number of women who have abortions are poor or are women of color. According to science writer Zara Abrams, "More than 60% of those who seek abortions are people of color and about half live below the federal poverty line."[2]

Surgical abortions are performed at a doctor's office or clinic. Up until about sixteen weeks of pregnancy, surgical abortions are performed by using suction to clear out a woman's uterus through her cervix. After sixteen weeks, surgical abortions are performed using dilation and evacuation, a procedure in which a medical professional dilates a woman's cervix and extracts the fetus using suction and medical instruments.

Medication abortions—also known as medical abortion or just "the abortion pill"—are an option up to about the tenth week of pregnancy. After meeting in person or remotely with a medical professional, patients are usually prescribed two drugs: mifepristone, a drug that causes an embryo to detach from the uterus, and misoprostol, a drug that clears out the uterus. (Occasionally, misoprostol is used alone in medication abortions.) Women usually take the drugs at home. This is a newer option that has only been available in the United States since 2000.

A Brief History of Abortion in the United States

Before the mid-1800s, abortion in the United States was unregulated. Women took herbs that were known to cause abortion, often under the care of a midwife. In the mid-1800s, a coalition of

doctors and Catholic clergy campaigned to make abortion illegal. By 1910 it was illegal across the country except when needed to save a woman's life. Some women opted for illegal abortions, which were dangerous and sometimes fatal.

In the 1960s organizations like the National Abortion Rights Action League and Planned Parenthood lobbied for the legalization of abortion. In the late 1960s and early 1970s, a few states—New York, Alaska, Hawaii, and Washington—repealed their abortion bans.

In 1973, in the landmark case *Roe v. Wade*, the Supreme Court ruled that a woman had a constitutional right to choose an abortion under the Fourteenth Amendment, which protects the right to privacy. According to the Supreme Court's decision, the constitutional right to privacy "is broad enough to encompass a woman's decision whether or not to terminate her pregnancy."[3]

The Abortion Debate After *Roe v. Wade*

After *Roe v. Wade*, abortion became a publicly divisive issue. While not all Americans are sure how they feel about abortion, the two main contrasting positions separate committed supporters into opposing camps dubbed pro-life and pro-choice.

The pro-life—or antiabortion—position maintains that abortion should be illegal in almost all cases. Proponents of this position believe that abortion is the murder of an unborn child and therefore a morally unacceptable act that should be banned. Many pro-life Americans are Christians who believe that abortion goes against their religious beliefs. Politically, most pro-life Americans are Republicans.

On the other hand, the pro-choice position argues that abortion should be legal in most cases. Proponents of this stance view abortion as a matter of women's rights, emphasizing that a woman should have autonomy over her body, including the decision to continue or terminate a pregnancy. Politically, most pro-choice Americans are Democrats.

Restrictions on Abortion

In the 1980s several Supreme Court cases made it possible for states to place restrictions on abortion, such as laws requiring minors to obtain parental permission for the procedure. Other states passed laws designed to encourage women to question their decision to have an abortion. For example, some states required women to meet with a counselor and then wait up to seventy-two hours to have the procedure.

By 2020 the Supreme Court had taken a conservative turn after the confirmation of several pro-life judges. This emboldened conservative states to pass even stricter abortion restrictions, like the 2021 Texas Heartbeat Law. In 2022 Idaho and Oklahoma passed similar laws.

Finally, on June 24, 2022, the Supreme Court overturned *Roe v. Wade*. In the *Dobbs v. Jackson Women's Health Organization* case, the Supreme Court decided that women did not have a constitutional right to an abortion. It was up to individual states to now decide whether abortion was legal within their borders.

The Abortion Debate After the End of *Roe v. Wade*

After the *Dobbs* decision, many states immediately enacted strict abortion laws. As of January 2024, abortion had been banned in fourteen states, with limited exceptions if the mother's life is in jeopardy. Two other states allow abortions only until six weeks, and two others until twelve weeks. In contrast, abortion remains legal in many states, and some states—like California, New Jersey, and Minnesota—have passed laws or state constitutional amendments to protect the right of women to obtain abortions.

The abortion issue continues to be hotly debated in courts and state legislatures. After *Roe v. Wade* was overturned, voters began to see abortion as one of the most important issues—and according to a Harvard University Institute of Politics poll, this is especially true for young voters.

The abortion issue is a complex one, and understanding the debates surrounding this issue is important so that the public can make informed decisions on how to vote. These debates include whether a woman should have the legal right to choose an abortion, whether medication abortion should be easily accessible, and whether abortion bans are dangerous.

Chapter One

Should Women Have the Legal Right to Choose Abortion?

Women Should Have the Legal Right to Choose Abortion

- Bodily autonomy is a human right.
- Abortion is a right-to-privacy issue.
- Control of reproduction is a tool of oppression.

Women Should Not Have the Legal Right to Choose Abortion

- Abortion kills a living human being.
- Human lives must be valued equally under the law.
- Individual rights are not limitless.

Women Should Have the Legal Right to Choose Abortion

"The debate about the legality of abortion should begin with that person's right to bodily autonomy even in the face of decisions that others might personally disagree with, or believe they would make differently."

—Monica Hesse, *Washington Post* columnist

Monica Hesse, "The One Point Abortion Rights Activists Need to Keep Making," *Washington Post*, October 3, 2022. www.washingtonpost.com.

Consider these questions as you read:

1. What restrictions (if any) do you think ought to be placed on abortion? Explain.
2. Are there situations in which it is okay to violate someone's bodily autonomy? If so, give examples. If not, why not?
3. What does the term *reproductive oppression* mean to you?

Editor's note: The discussion that follows presents common arguments made in support of this perspective, reinforced by facts, quotes, and examples taken from various sources.

Women must have the legal right to choose an abortion because in a free society, laws protect fundamental freedoms. These include the freedom for individuals to control their own bodies. Pro-life advocates believe that a woman loses the right to control her body when she becomes pregnant. Pro-choice advocates believe this is a violation of a pregnant woman's right to bodily autonomy.

Bodily Autonomy

The United Nations Population Fund (UNFPA) defines bodily autonomy as "the power and agency to make choices over one's body . . . without violence or coercion."[4] According to Natalia Kanem, executive director of the UNFPA, "The Universal

Declaration of Human Rights and other international human rights agreements underscore that bodily autonomy is a fundamental right."[5]

Forcing a woman to remain pregnant is an especially problematic violation of bodily autonomy because of the physical and emotional toll that pregnancy takes on a woman's body. Even in normal pregnancies, women struggle with chronic symptoms like fatigue, nausea, heartburn, and depression. More serious risks include infections, diabetes, and dangerously high blood pressure. Moreover, while childbirth-related deaths are now uncommon, they still happen. In 2021 the US maternal death rate was about 33 deaths per 1,000 live births—and about 70 deaths per 1,000 live births for Black women. Pregnancy is challenging enough for women who want to be pregnant, but forcing a woman to go through this is inhumane.

Pro-life advocates argue that it is necessary to compromise a woman's bodily autonomy when she is pregnant with another living being. However, as women's rights activists Kathryn Kolbert and Julie F. Kay argue, it is inhumane to force individuals to sacrifice their body to help others. "Our laws do not require anyone to donate a kidney to save the life of a family member," they argue. "Parents are not mandated to donate blood or bone marrow to save their children."[6] Doctors cannot even donate the organs of a deceased person to save another person's life unless the deceased gave prior permission.

Bodily Autonomy and the Right to Privacy

The right to bodily autonomy overlaps with an individual's right to privacy. In a free society there is a difference between how the government handles public matters versus private matters. Public matters—like whether a city will spend taxpayers' money to build a new school—are issues that impact the community. Government officials and voters have a say when it comes to decisions like this. However, when a matter is private, the government and the public do not have a say. Adults can make decisions that impact their bodies—like getting a tattoo or a vaccine—and the government and the public cannot interfere because these are private decisions.

Similarly, the decision to have an abortion is a strictly private matter, regardless of how government officials or the neighbors feel about it. In fact, the right to privacy was the basis for *Roe v Wade*. As Supreme Court justice William J. Brennan Jr. argued in a related Supreme Court case, "If the right to privacy means anything, it is the right of the individual, married or single, to be free from unwanted government intrusion into matters so fundamentally affecting a person as the decision to bear or beget a child."[7]

Abortion Does Not Conflict with Religious Freedom

Another right that overlaps with bodily autonomy is freedom of religion. The pro-life movement has been strongly influenced by Christian activists and politicians who believe that abortion should be illegal because they disagree with it for religious reasons. Since the 1970s, when the movement gained prominence through right-wing religious groups like the Moral Majority, many politicians have unapologetically interjected their religious beliefs into the abortion issue. Mississippi representative Cindy Hyde-Smith, for instance, asserts on her website, "Cindy believes every child, including the unborn, is entitled to the right to life bestowed by our Creator."[8]

If a pregnant woman feels that abortion goes against her religious beliefs, she can choose not to have an abortion. This is an exercise of her bodily autonomy. However, her beliefs do not give her the right to take away the bodily autonomy of another woman. The First Amendment of the Constitution states, "Congress shall make no law respecting an establishment of religion, or prohibiting

Strong Support for Legal Abortion

When asked for their views on whether abortion should be legal, 64 percent of poll respondents said they believe that abortion should be legal in all or most cases. This was the finding of a 2023 AP-NORC poll that sought to gauge public attitudes a year after *Roe v. Wade* was overturned by the US Supreme Court.

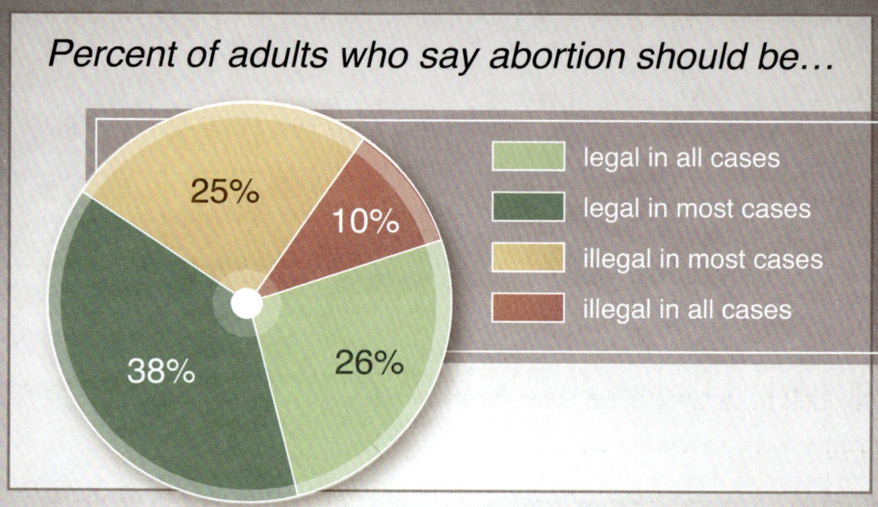

Source: "Most Americans Support Legal Abortion with Some Restrictions," AP-NORC, July 12, 2023. www.apnorc.org.

the free exercise thereof."[9] This means that the government cannot pass laws that favor one religion over any other.

However, the purpose of the pro-life movement is to pass abortion laws that all women must follow regardless of their beliefs. This is unfair both to nonbelievers and to religious Americans who hold different beliefs about abortion. For example, in Judaism, abortion is a moral requirement if a mother's life is in danger, and the Reform and Conservative Jewish denominations are officially pro-choice. Moreover, pro-life views are not even held by all Christians. According to a 2022 Pew Research Center poll, 66 percent of Black Protestants, 60 percent of non-evangelical White Protestants, and 56 percent of Catholics believe abortion should be legal in all or almost all cases.

It is unconstitutional to make laws based on religious beliefs. Besides, the United States is not a theocracy where the legal system is based on religious law. The world's theocracies include Iran, Afghanistan, and Saudi Arabia—countries where women and religious minorities are oppressed. Banning abortion because of religious beliefs is a move toward theocracy, and the laws of the United States prohibit this. America's laws must preserve the liberties guaranteed to all citizens.

Reproductive Oppression

The opposite of liberty is oppression, and the opposite of bodily autonomy is reproductive oppression. The Women's Leadership and Resource Center at the University of Illinois–Chicago defines reproductive oppression as "the regulation and exploitation of individuals' bodies, sexuality, labor, and procreative capacities as a strategy to control individuals and entire communities."[10]

Abortion bans are a form of reproductive oppression because they exert control over women's bodies, and as a result, women are less empowered to participate in society as equals.

"The ability to decide whether and when to become pregnant and parent is crucial to determining one's own life's path, pursuing personal and professional goals, and safeguarding economic security," argues the National Women's Law Center. "Access to abortion enables women to complete high school and higher levels of education, improves labor force participation, and enables economic independence."[11]

> "The ability to decide whether and when to become pregnant and parent is crucial to determining one's own life's path, pursuing personal and professional goals, and safeguarding economic security."[11]
>
> —National Women's Law Center

Abortion bans are especially dangerous because of the historical precedent of using reproductive oppression to exert control over women in gruesome ways. During the twentieth century a common form of reproductive oppression was forced sterilization, a medical procedure that takes away a woman's fertility. This was used in Canada and Australia to reduce indigenous populations. It was also common in the United States. In 1927 the Supreme Court decided it was legal to forcibly sterilize women if doctors diagnosed them as "feebleminded." This led to the sterilization of up to seventy thousand women, most of whom were women of color or women with disabilities. White doctors used these sterilizations to control populations they considered inferior. "They sterilized me directly after giving birth without my consent," recounts Elaine Riddick, a Black woman who gave birth when she was fourteen after being raped in 1968. "I was dehumanized and treated like a hog or some domesticated animal."[12]

In a free society, governments need to protect women from reproductive oppression by preserving their right to bodily autonomy. The law must allow women to exercise their right to privacy and their right to make decisions that reflect their personal religious beliefs.

Women Should Not Have the Legal Right to Choose Abortion

"I am pro-life because even if the Bible did not indisputably tell me so, the plain undisputed facts of science also tell me so."

—Tim Counts, pastor of Northshire Baptist Church in Manchester Center, Vermont

Tim Counts, "3 Compelling Reasons I Am Pro-life," Ethics of Religious Liberty Commission, July 12, 2022. www.eric.com.

Consider these questions as you read:

1. Do you think an unborn child is a person? What evidence supports your answer?
2. How compelling is the argument that the right of an unborn child to life is more important than the mother's right to bodily autonomy? Explain.
3. How compelling is the argument that unborn children should have the same legal rights as other human beings? Explain.

Editor's note: The discussion that follows presents common arguments made in support of this perspective, reinforced by facts, quotes, and examples taken from various sources.

Perhaps the most important pro-life argument is the simplest: an unborn child is a living human being. Laws must not permit the killing of human beings. "All human beings have basic, natural rights," writes the Heritage Foundation, a conservative think tank. "The most fundamental of these is the right to life. . . . Government should protect the right to life because it is the foundation of all other liberties."[13]

The Humanness of an Unborn Child

An unborn child is a living human being from the moment of conception. This is a scientific fact. Almost all biologists agree that life begins when an egg is fertilized by a sperm cell. In 2021 the scientific journal *Issues in Law & Medicine* published the results of a survey of over five thousand biologists from over one thousand academic institutions. Ninety-six percent of these biologists said that life begins when an egg is fertilized.

Unborn children begin to develop human characteristics and bodily structure quickly. According to WebMD, a medical website, the heart, blood vessels, lungs, and stomach of an unborn child start to develop in the fourth week of pregnancy. By eight weeks, the unborn child has arms, legs, and eyes. By sixteen weeks, an unborn child looks like a tiny baby. According to the Cleveland Clinic, a major medical provider, "The 16-week-old unborn child has lips and its ears are developed enough that it can hear you talk. Even though its eyes are closed, the fetus can react to light by turning away from it."[14] According to WebMD, an unborn child can feel pain at twenty-four weeks—and possibly as early as twelve weeks.

Unborn children are equally alive and human before and after they are born. "There is no magical birth canal that moves a preborn from being a non-human, non-alive entity to human and alive,"[15] argues Danielle Pitzer of Focus on the Family, a pro-life Christian organization. Killing a baby is one of the most horrific crimes imaginable, and it is equally horrific to kill an unborn child who has not yet left its mother's body.

A Separate and Unique Life

Because an unborn child is a living human being, the pro-choice argument about the need to protect a woman's bodily autonomy is invalid. When a woman is pregnant, there are two separate bodies involved. From the moment an egg is fertilized, a new person is formed with a complete and unique genetic blueprint that is different from the mother's. "Sperm and egg, by themselves, only contain half the genetic material needed to form a human being," explains Live Action, a pro-life advocacy organization. "When these cells fuse, however, a new individual who is genetically distinct from both parents comes into existence."[16]

A woman's bodily autonomy does not extend to her unborn child because the child is simply not a part of her body. As the pro-life website Abort73 argues, "No matter how you spin it, women don't have four arms and four legs when they're pregnant. Those extra appendages belong to the tiny human being(s) living inside of them. At *no* point in pregnancy is the developing embryo or fetus simply a part of the mother's body."[17]

The S.L.E.D. Test Indicates That the Unborn Should Have Equality Under the Law

Because unborn children are living human beings, they deserve the same rights as other living human beings. The Universal Declaration of Human Rights—one of the world's most authoritative human rights documents—states, "All are equal before the law and are entitled without any discrimination to equal protection of the law."[18]

Treating one person as less valuable under the law is a human rights violation. Because unborn children are human beings, treating them as less valuable under the law is also a human rights violation. In most cases the law punishes people severely if they kill another person, but these laws are not applied equally to unborn children. This is illustrated by what pro-life activists call the S.L.E.D. test—a concept originally developed by Stephen Schwartz and adapted by Scott Klusendorf. The "test" asks questions about the value of human life.

In the S.L.E.D. test, the *S* stands for "size." People who are small are not seen as less valuable before the law than larger people, so why should the tiny unborn be considered too small to be valued equally? The *L* stands for "level of development." Children are physically and intellectually less developed than adults, but they are not seen as less valuable, so why should the unborn be seen as less valuable because they are not fully developed? The *E* stands for "environment." A person's humanity stays the same no matter what environment he or she is in—at home, on a beach, on a mountain, and so forth—so why should an unborn child's humanity be seen as less valuable inside the womb than outside it? The *D* stands for "degree of dependency." Young children are not seen as less valuable because of their dependency on others, so why should the unborn be considered less valuable because they are dependent on their mother's body?

Individual Rights Are Not Limitless

Because an unborn child is a human being, a pregnant woman loses the absolute right to her bodily autonomy. This is the case in any situation in which one person's individual rights harm another person. Although individual rights are an important part of freedom, they are not limitless. When the exercise of one person's rights harms another person, limits must be placed on these rights.

One example of this is parenting. Parents have the right to raise their children as they see fit, regardless of the opinions of others. They can raise their children according to their spiritual beliefs and values. However, the individual rights of the parents can be taken away if they physically abuse their children. The government can remove children from a home in which they are being harmed.

As Abort73 explains, when two people's rights are at odds with each other, the rights of the person with the most to lose need to be respected—especially if what they have to lose is their life. For example, drivers must stop when pedestrians cross the street in front of them. A driver's individual right to drive freely is less important than a pedestrian's right to cross the street safely.

Abortion Should Not Be an Unfettered Right

Many Americans do not favor abortion on demand. According to a Pew Research Center poll, 56 percent of US adults say that the stage of pregnancy should determine whether a woman can obtain a legal abortion. The percentage who share this view is slightly lower for women and slightly higher for men but still amounts to more than half for these groups.

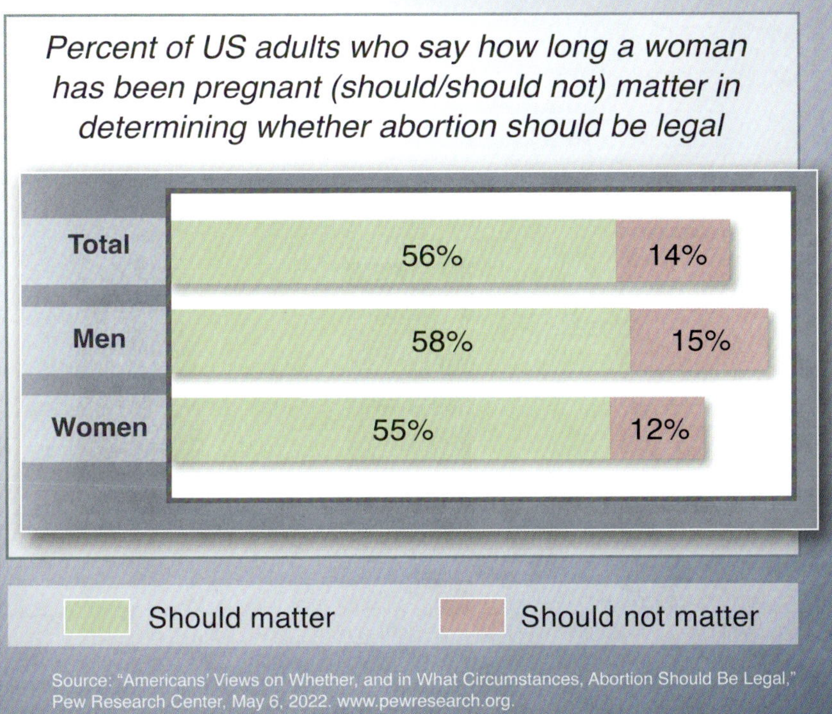

Source: "Americans' Views on Whether, and in What Circumstances, Abortion Should Be Legal," Pew Research Center, May 6, 2022. www.pewresearch.org.

This is not because the pedestrian is more important but because the pedestrian has more to lose. The inconvenience of the driver is less important than the right of the pedestrian to live.

While it is true that being pregnant is more difficult than being an inconvenienced driver, the same is true in the case of pregnancy: the unborn child has more to lose than the mother. Although the mother may struggle physically and financially—quite a bit, in some cases—the unborn child stands to lose more. "Abortion costs the unborn child his or her very life, and it is a thoroughly permanent condition," argues Abort73. "This is what's at stake for the two parties most directly involved. It is not an issue of who is more important, but rather who has more on the line."[19]

An unplanned pregnancy can be extremely challenging, and this should not be minimized. However, when it comes to the conflicting rights of bodily autonomy and life, life is simply more important. Without question, unborn children are living human beings who are distinct from their mother, and laws need to protect life above all else.

Chapter Two

Should Medication Abortion Be Easily Accessible?

Medication Abortion Should Be Easily Accessible

- Medication abortion is safe.
- Medication abortion improves access to abortion.
- Medication abortion gives women a choice of procedures.

Medication Abortion Should Not Be Easily Accessible

- Medication abortions can be painful and cause dangerous complications.
- Medication abortions increase the likelihood of incomplete abortions.
- Abortion pills are too easy to access without a prescription.

Medication Abortion Should Be Easily Accessible

"I had an abortion in October of last year while I was on tour. I went to Planned Parenthood where they gave me the abortion pill. It was easy. Everyone deserves that kind of access."

—Phoebe Bridgers, singer/songwriter

Phoebe Bridgers (@phoebe_bridgers), "I had an abortion in October of last year . . . " X, May 3, 2022, 3:08 p.m. https://twitter.com/phoebe_bridgers/status/1521582506801254400.

Consider these questions as you read:

1. Based on this discussion, how persuasive is the argument that medication abortion is safe? Explain.
2. What are some advantages and disadvantages of doctors using virtual medical appointments to prescribe abortion pills to patients?
3. Considering the facts and ideas presented in this discussion, how persuasive is the argument that women ought to be able to choose between surgical and medication abortion? Explain.

Editor's note: The discussion that follows presents common arguments made in support of this perspective, reinforced by facts, quotes, and examples taken from various sources.

Since *Roe v. Wade* was overturned, pro-life groups have been challenging the use of mifepristone—the primary drug used in medication abortions—in court. Their main argument is that the drug is unsafe. In December 2023 the Supreme Court agreed to review a case that could allow states to limit or ban the use of mifepristone. These lawsuits do not have merit, because although medication abortion can be very painful, it is very safe. The drug misoprostol, which is used to clear out the uterus after a woman has taken mifepristone, has also been proved safe to use. If the true goal of pro-life groups is to protect women from an unsafe drug—as opposed to simply making it harder for women to get abortions—then placing limits on mifepristone is pointless.

The Safety of Abortion Pills

A team of *New York Times* reporters, in consultation with medical consultants, reviewed 101 medical studies on medication abortion. These studies took place over the course of more than thirty years in twenty-six different countries. The reporters concluded, "More than 100 scientific studies, spanning continents and decades, have examined the effectiveness and safety of mifepristone and misoprostol, the abortion pills that are commonly used in the United States. All conclude that the pills are a safe method for terminating a pregnancy."[20]

According to the studies analyzed by the *New York Times*, over 99 percent of women and girls who took abortion pills had no serious complications. Moreover, according to a Supreme Court brief filed by organizations such as the American Medical Association (AMA) and the American College of Obstetricians and Gynecologists (ACOG), the mortality rate of medication abortion is minuscule.

> "More than 100 scientific studies . . . have examined the effectiveness and safety of . . . the abortion pills that are commonly used in the United States. All conclude that the pills are a safe method for terminating a pregnancy."[20]
>
> —A 2023 *New York Times* report on the safety of abortion pills

While all drugs come with potential side effects, serious side effects of mifepristone are rare. A CNN analysis of medical studies concluded that "mifepristone is even safer than some common, low-risk prescription drugs, including penicillin [an antibiotic] and Viagra [an erectile dysfunction medication]."[21] In fact, abortions of all kinds are safer than many common medical procedures. According to the Supreme Court brief filed by the AMA and ACOG, "There is a greater risk of complications or mortality from procedures like wisdom-tooth removals, tonsillectomies, colonoscopies, and plastic surgeries, than by any abortion method."[22]

Many More Women Must Now Travel for Abortions

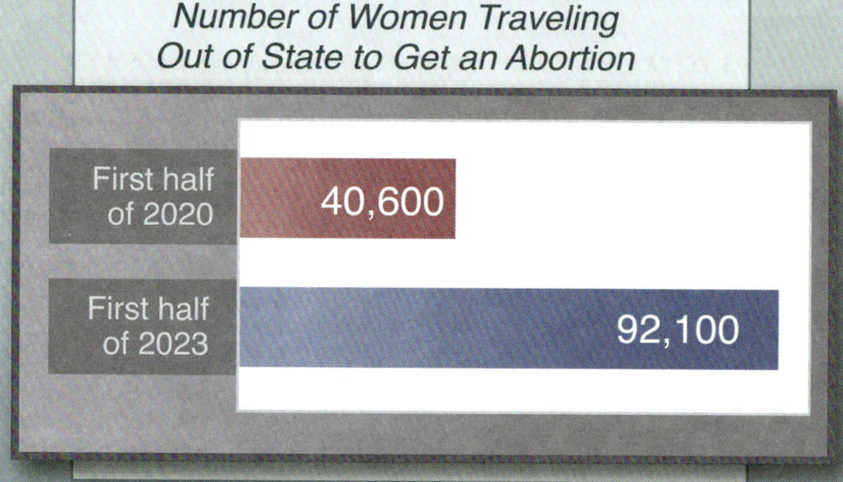

Source: Kimya Forouzan et al., "The High Toll of US Abortion Bans: Nearly One in Five Patients Now Traveling Out of State for Abortion Care," Guttmacher Institute, December 7, 2023. www.guttmacher.org.

The *New York Times* analysis does show a slightly higher risk of serious complications for medication abortion (0.31 percent) compared to surgical abortion (0.16 percent). However, medication abortions have a safety advantage because surgical abortion comes with a minor risk of injury to the cervix or uterus. Both kinds of abortion are less risky than childbirth, which has a 1.4 percent chance of serious complication.

Improving Abortion Access

Since medication abortion is safe, there is no reason not to make it widely accessible, especially because availability of these drugs benefits women in several ways. One way medication abortion is beneficial is that it improves access to abortion. As the American Civil Liberties Union argues, "Due to its accessibility via telehealth and mail delivery, it plays a critical role in ensuring safe and timely access to care for people who live far away from the nearest abortion provider or face long wait-times for an in-person appointment."[23]

Telehealth plays an important role in the accessibility of medication abortion. A patient meets with a medical provider remotely, and afterward, the provider mails the drugs directly to the patient or calls in a prescription to a pharmacy. Many clinics provide telehealth appointments, as do organizations like Aid Access, which exclusively provide medication abortion via virtual appointments.

The availability of medication abortions via telehealth is crucial because even in states where abortion is legal, clinics that perform surgical abortions are scarce. For example, abortion is legal in Minnesota, but there are only eight surgical abortion providers in the state. Because of the scarcity of abortion clinics, women in rural areas may have to drive for hours for an abortion. This can be cost-prohibitive for women who lack transportation or cannot get time off from work. In addition, the scarcity of clinics often means long waits for appointments. This is especially true since the repeal of *Roe v. Wade* because women from states where abortion is illegal are making appointments in and traveling to states where it is legal.

Another way that medication abortion increases access is that it is often cheaper than surgical abortion. Although medication abortions and first-trimester surgical abortions cost about the same at a clinic—at Planned Parenthood, these cost roughly $500 to $800—online medication abortion services cost less. For example, Aid Access charges $150 for a medication abortion. Moreover, post-reversal of *Roe v. Wade*, surgical abortion has become very expensive for women who must travel out of state for this procedure. Transportation, a hotel room, missed work, and other expenses can cost thousands of dollars.

Increasing Women's Choice of Procedures

In addition to increasing accessibility to abortion, medication abortion is also beneficial because it gives women a choice of procedures. For example, women can choose to give birth at a hospital, a midwife center, or their home—whichever setting they prefer. The same is true of abortion.

The ability to choose between surgical and medication abortion is especially important because for most women, abortion is a personal and emotional experience. Different women have different needs. "Some people like surgical, because it's over with faster, they're able to have anesthesia, and it's finished in a defined time," explains Dr. Maria Isabel Rodriguez, a professor of obstetrics and gynecology. "Medication can feel more private, some want it at their own home, some say it feels more natural for them, and some say it feels more possible to process a loss."[24]

Women who have chosen medication abortions confirm these views. Maya, a woman who chose medication abortion, explains, "It was so nice to be able to do it in the comfort of my own home and to have my partner be able to be there too."[25] Another woman, who prefers to remain anonymous, comments, "To be able to go through that process in my own space on my own time and have a little bit more control was really empowering."[26]

The privacy of medication abortion is appealing for many women. They do not want to be surrounded by strangers at a clinic or deal with pro-life demonstrators, who often protest outside clinics. Some also worry about being recognized. "You can walk into a Planned Parenthood clinic, and they are wonderful places, but you can't guarantee that you're not going to see your neighbor or that your boss isn't going to drive by,"[27] explains Stephanie.

> "It was so nice to be able to [take an abortion pill] in the comfort of my own home and to have my partner be able to be there too."[25]
>
> —Maya, a woman who had a medication abortion

In contrast, other women choose surgical abortion. Many do so because medical abortions are sometimes very painful, especially for women who are close to the ten-week cutoff. Others feel more at ease having the procedure done by a professional and appreciate the supportive atmosphere that many clinics offer. "I was a nervous kid who had no idea what to expect, and I was treated with nothing but absolute respect by everyone from the receptionist to the doctor to the nurses in post-op,"[28] explains Alyssa.

Abortion is a personal choice. Just as women should be able to choose between abortion and childbirth, women should have the freedom to choose between medication and surgical abortion. If they choose medication abortion—a procedure that has been proved to be safe—they should be able to access it easily.

"What women aren't told about the risks of DIY abortion pills can seriously harm them, including complications like hemorrhage, infection, need for surgery or even death."

—Marjorie Dannenfelser, president of Susan B. Anthony Pro-Life America

Quoted in Susan B. Anthony Pro-Life America, "Shame on Dems & Media: Mail-Order Abortion Pills Are Not Legal or Safe," Susan B. Anthony Pro-Life America, July 20, 2023. www.sbaprolife.org.

Consider these questions as you read:

1. Do you think it is fair to ban abortion pills in all states, including those where abortion is legal? Why or why not?
2. After reading over the potential complications of medication abortion listed in this discussion, what side effects do you think should be considered serious, and which should not? Explain.
3. Could you justify buying abortion drugs without a prescription? Explain your answer.

Editor's note: The discussion that follows presents common arguments made in support of this perspective, reinforced by facts, quotes, and examples taken from various sources.

The pills used for medication abortion should not be easily accessible. Pro-choice advocates have downplayed the dangerous complications that can come with a medication abortion. This downplaying is apparent in the 2023 summary of research on medication abortion in the *New York Times*.

Dangerous Complications

According to the *New York Times*, only about 0.31 percent of women who had medication abortions had serious complications. This claim oversimplifies the dangerous potential complications of medication abortion. For one thing, while 0.31 is a low percentage, it is important to consider how many women that number represents. According to the Guttmacher Institute's estimate that 53 percent of the country's 930,160 abortions were medication abortions in 2020, that means over 1,500 women suffered serious complications in 2020 alone.

What is especially misleading is that the *New York Times*'s definition of serious complications is narrow. The publication only considers a complication to be serious if it "might cause permanent damage to health without medical intervention,"[29] including infections that are serious enough to cause hospitalization and blood loss that is severe enough to require a blood transfusion.

However, there are potentially serious complications that the *New York Times* placed in the category of moderate complications. This includes uterine infections that are serious enough to require antibiotics. In fact, uterine infections that are serious enough to require antibiotics can lead to sepsis, which pharmacist Alyssa Billingsley defines as "a life-threatening response to an infection in your body."[30]

The Risks of Incomplete Abortions

The *New York Times* also placed incomplete abortions into the moderate complications category. An incomplete abortion is one in which the procedure fails to remove all the fetal tissue from the uterus. This can potentially lead to very serious bleeding and infection—and usually means that the woman will need a surgical procedure to clear out her uterus.

If the *New York Times* had included incomplete abortions in the serious complications category, the 0.31 statistic would have been much higher—because incomplete abortions are not rare. According to Planned Parenthood, they happen about 1 percent of the time after a surgical abortion. After a medication abortion, the rate is 2 to 6 percent for abortions that take place in the first eight weeks of pregnancy. Medication abortions that take place between ten and eleven weeks have a 2 percent rate if a woman takes an extra dose of misoprostol, but if not, the rate is up to 13 percent.

Assuming that at least 2 percent of women have incomplete abortions after a medication abortion, then according to Guttmacher Institute statistics, that equates to over ninety-eight hundred women who had incomplete abortions in 2020 alone. Incomplete abortion is not rare, and the *New York Times*'s claim that serious effects of medication abortion are rare is an oversimplification.

Extreme Pain and Heavy Blood Flow

In addition to the risk of incomplete abortion, medication abortions frequently cause excruciating pain and heavy bleeding. In a study published in the academic journal *Contraception* in 2022, 38 percent of participants suffered from severe pain after a medication abortion. While severe pain may not be life threatening, it can be a traumatic experience. Medication abortion may sound like a simple matter of taking pills to end a pregnancy. But there is nothing simple about severe pain and bleeding, and for many women, this is the reality.

Almost all women who have medication abortions experience at least some pain and blood loss. Most of the pain is caused by misoprostol, which causes the uterus to contract and expel the embryo or fetus. As the uterus clears out, blood is expelled, sometimes in large clots, and the woman experiences painful cramps.

The amount of pain and blood loss varies. Some women experience mild cramps and relatively light blood flow, but others can have agonizing cramps and blood flow that can last for over a week. The amount of pain and blood usually increases the further along a woman is in her pregnancy. "I was not prepared for how much pain I would be in,"[31] says Layidua Salazar, a woman who had a medication abortion at ten weeks. Salazar was told the pain would be similar to the discomfort of menstrual cramps, but it was significantly worse. She was in bed with debilitating cramps for three days—even after taking the strong prescription painkillers she was prescribed—and the pain continued for over a week.

Jessica, who was seven weeks pregnant when she had a medication abortion, was also told that the pain would be minor. But after taking the pills, she experienced pain more severe than when she had given birth a few years prior. "I couldn't leave the toilet, or be without a bowl at all times for the vomiting," explains Jessica. "I was just curled up on the bathroom floor, sobbing. It was horrible. . . . Then the cramping and bleeding continued on for about three weeks afterwards."[32]

—Jessica, a woman who had a medication abortion

The Danger of Easy Access

Because of serious and painful side effects of medication abortion, abortion pills should not be distributed without a prescription and the guidance of a medical professional. However, this is not always the case. Abortion pills have become way too easy to access without a prescription. Ideally, they should be banned, but if that is not possible, the government needs to regulate them heavily to prevent women from using these potentially dangerous medications on their own.

One way that women can get abortion pills without a prescription is through the mail. As of January 2024, it was not illegal in many states to mail abortion pills—even to states where abortion is illegal. In addition to making it easier for women to get abortion pills without a prescription, mail-order pill delivery makes it harder for states to enforce antiabortion laws, which they are entitled to do following the 2022 *Dobbs* Supreme Court decision.

Medication Abortions Can Lead to a Dangerous Complication

Pro-choice advocates argue that there are rarely serious complications from medication abortion, but this is untrue. Incomplete abortion—a dangerous condition where tissue remains in a woman's uterus after an abortion—is common. Women who have incomplete abortions are at risk for deadly infections and usually need a surgical procedure. A woman who has a medication abortion when she is 9 or 10 weeks pregnant has almost a 7 percent chance of having an incomplete abortion. This is just one reason why medication abortions should not be easy to obtain.

Week of Pregnancy	Likelihood of Incomplete Abortion after a Medication Abortion
7 weeks or less	1.9 %
7–8 weeks	3.3%
8–9 weeks	4.8%
9–10 weeks	6.9%

Source: Ingrid Skop, "No-Test Chemical Abortion Provision: Can It Be Justified?," Charlotte Lozier Institute, April 28, 2022. www.lozierinstitute.org.

Another way that women can get abortion pills without a prescription is through the online black market. This shady industry has grown since it became harder for women in many states to get abortion pill prescriptions. "Counterfeit criminals go to where there's demand—and there's demand and there's access challenges," says Libby Baney of Alliance for Safe Online Pharmacies. "That creates criminal opportunity and a major patient safety risk."[33] The black market has led to price gouging, with some sellers charging significantly more than what the drugs cost legally because women are turning to whatever supplier they can find. There is no guarantee that the drugs that are sold on the black market are not expired or counterfeit, and these possibilities lead to potential dangers for the health of desperate buyers.

The accessibility of abortion pills also makes it easier for minors to acquire them, even without parental consent. "The abortion clinic of today and tomorrow is your neighbor's teenage daughter's bathroom,"[34] says Roxy Lamorgese, executive director of the pro-life organization PreBorn! Providing these drugs to minors is especially dangerous because they might lack information about how to use abortion drugs correctly. They also may not know that it is dangerous to use the drugs after ten weeks of pregnancy, and they might fail to recognize when they have had an incomplete abortion after trusting in the drugs.

Medication abortion, if it exists at all, needs to become much less accessible. The procedure is potentially dangerous and often extremely painful. The government must prevent women and girls from getting these pills without a prescription.

Chapter Three

Are Abortion Bans Harmful to Women?

Abortion Bans Are Harmful to Women

- If women cannot get legal abortions, they will get dangerous illegal abortions.
- Abortion bans make it harder for women to get an abortion when necessary to save their lives.
- Abortion bans make it harder for women to escape reproductive coercion.

Abortion Bans Are Not Harmful to Women

- Abortion bans allow exceptions for the life of the mother.
- Abortion bans protect women from abortion coercion.
- Women are harmed by issues like financial insecurity that cause them to get abortions—not by abortion bans.

Abortion Bans Are Harmful to Women

"I have lived in a world where abortion was illegal. I learned early on that when the law bans all abortions, only safe and legal abortions will be banned. I lived in a world in which women bled to death from back alley abortions. A world in which infections and other complications destroyed women's futures. . . . Changes in abortion laws will have dire consequences."

—Elizabeth Warren, US senator from Massachusetts

Elizabeth Warren, "Elizabeth Warren: I Am Angry but Determined to Protect *Roe*," *Marie Claire*, May 9, 2022. www.marieclaire.com.

Consider these questions as you read:

1. Considering the facts and ideas presented in this discussion, how persuasive is the argument that abortion bans are harmful to women? Explain your answer.
2. In states where abortion is illegal in most cases, what are some reasons why doctors might not be willing to perform an abortion that is needed to save a woman's life?
3. Do you think the term *reproductive coercion* is an accurate term to describe pressuring a woman to not have an abortion? Why or why not?

Editor's note: The discussion that follows presents common arguments made in support of this perspective, reinforced by facts, quotes, and examples taken from various sources.

In 1968, before *Roe v. Wade*, college sophomore Phyllis was pregnant. She contacted a doctor who had a reputation for providing illegal abortions safely. But then the doctor called and said he had heard that the police were going to raid his office. He said he would still do the abortion, but it would have to be without anesthesia and in a motel room instead of his clinic. Phyllis agreed. The experience was horrific. Phyllis writes:

> I've never felt pain like that, not before, nor since. I wasn't allowed to yell for fear of being heard through the walls. I have no idea how long the procedure was, but it felt like hours. When it was finally over, he handed me a vitamin K pill, and I slept curled up on a chair for 20 minutes. Then he drove me back to the hotel where he dropped me on the sidewalk like a pile of dirty clothes. I felt brutally tortured! There is no other way to describe this experience. I felt degraded and ashamed, forced to endure something I never would have imagined.[35]

Abortion bans harm women because they place their health and lives at risk. One way they do so is by removing the option of safe, legal abortions, which will cause women like Phyllis who have no other options to seek dangerous, illegal abortions.

Illegal Abortions Spread When Abortion Is Banned

Worldwide, whenever abortion has been made illegal, many women have chosen to undergo dangerous illegal abortions to avoid giving birth. This was true in the United States before *Roe v. Wade*. The Guttmacher Institute estimates that there were 200,000 to 1.2 million illegal abortions in the United States during the 1950s and 1960s. In 1965, 17 percent of maternal deaths related to pregnancy were caused by illegal abortions—and that only includes the deaths that were reported. Maternal deaths were disproportionally high for women of color, as were hospitalizations for complications. After *Roe v.*

Wade, the Centers for Disease Control and Prevention reported a 45 percent decrease in maternal deaths from 1972 to 1974.

It is hard to measure how many illegal abortions have happened since *Roe v. Wade* was overturned. However, international studies indicate a strong correlation between abortion bans and illegal abortions. "Many studies have shown that making abortions illegal doesn't decline the number of abortions," says Harvard University reproductive health expert Ana Langer. "Once a procedure becomes illegal, the need is still there. Women will look for services, safe or unsafe, to terminate their pregnancy."[36]

The Threat to Women Who Need Emergency Abortions

Another way that abortion bans harm women is by making it harder for women to get abortions they need to save their lives. One woman who almost died because of the abortion ban in Texas was Amanda Zurawski. In 2022, after a year of fertility treatments, Zurawski was ecstatic to be pregnant. But at eighteen weeks, her water broke, which meant there was no way her fetus could survive. Zurawski was in danger of getting a deadly infection, and the safest thing for her to do was to get an abortion.

But Texas only allowed abortion if a mother's life was in danger. There was a good chance Zurawski's life would be in danger, but because her life was not in danger immediately after her water broke, doctors were unwilling to risk breaking the law by giving her an abortion. They told her to go home and come back if she got sick enough to die—which is exactly what she did. She contracted an uncontrollable infection that was so bad that family members flew in to say good-bye. Zurawski did survive, but she may not be able to get pregnant again.

Even though states like Texas have exceptions for medical emergencies, they are worded vaguely. Many obstetricians and gynecologists (OB-GYNs) are unwilling to provide emergency abortions if there is any chance that they are breaking the law. According to the independent polling agency KFF, "Nationally, one in five office-based OB-GYNs (20%) report they have personally felt constraints on their ability to provide care for miscarriages and other pregnancy-related medical emergencies since the *Dobbs* decision. In states where abortion is banned, this share rises to four in ten OB-GYNs (40%)."[37]

Along with the Center for Reproductive Rights, Zurawski filed a lawsuit against the state of Texas, demanding that the state clarify the medical emergency exception to its abortion law. And because her case was not unique, twenty-one additional women with similar experiences joined the lawsuit. Oral arguments for the case were presented in November 2023. A decision was expected by June 2024.

Abortion bans have also impacted the ability for women to be treated for miscarriages. In July 2022 a Wisconsin woman had an incomplete miscarriage, which means fetal tissue was left behind after she miscarried. However, because of the vague wording of the state abortion ban, doctors feared they could be in legal jeopardy if they cleared out her uterus—even though the fetus was deceased. They refused to treat the incomplete miscarriage until after she had bled for ten days.

These instances show that abortion bans are preventing women from getting lifesaving medical care. Such outcomes also undermine counterarguments that purport to value life. As Amanda Zurawski's husband, Josh, stated, "Amanda almost died. That's not pro-life."[38]

Reproductive Coercion

Abortion bans are also dangerous to women because they make it harder for them to escape a type of domestic violence called reproductive coercion, which is when individuals attempt to control their partner's reproductive autonomy. Examples of this include sabotaging a woman's birth control or pressuring her either to get an abortion or not get one. Men can be victims too, like when a woman falsely claims to be taking birth control pills so she can

Nationwide Abortion Ban Would Increase Maternal Mortality Rate

The US maternal mortality rate is among the highest in the industrialized world—more than ten times the rate of countries such as Australia, Japan, and Spain. A nationwide abortion ban would likely increase the maternal death rate. A University of Colorado study estimates that a nationwide ban would result in a 24 percent rise in pregnancy-related deaths for all women and a 39 percent rise in pregnancy-related deaths for Black women. One reason for this is that pregnancy-related deaths are far more common than abortion-related deaths—so if more women are pregnant because they cannot get abortions, more will die.

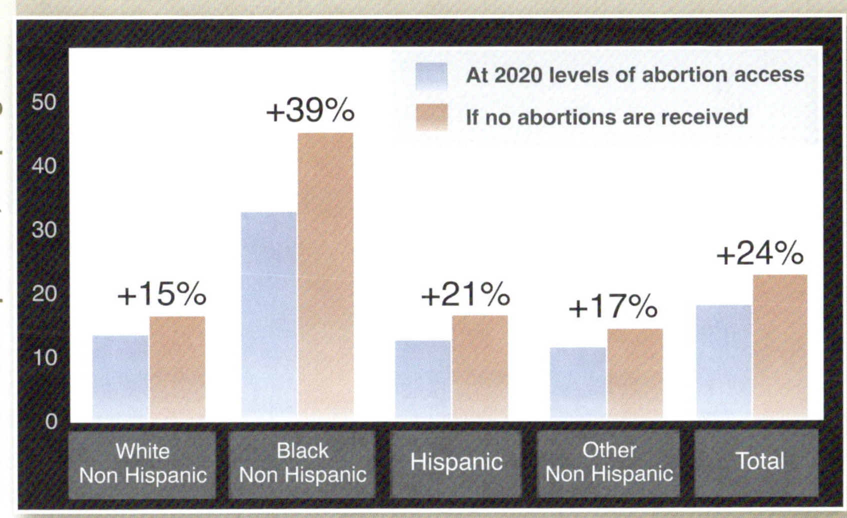

Source: Amanda Jean Stevenson et al., "The Maternal Mortality Consequences of Losing Abortion Access," SocArXiv Papers, June 29, 2022. https://osf.io/preprints/socarxiv/7g29k.

get pregnant against a man's wishes. According to the National Domestic Violence Hotline, about one in four of its callers in 2021 said they were experiencing reproductive coercion, often in conjunction with physical and emotional abuse.

For women in relationships who are being reproductively coerced, abortion bans can make it harder to avoid unwanted consequences. Some male partners use reproductive coercion to make a woman stay in an abusive relationship because the woman may be financially dependent on the man and lack the resources to raise a baby on her own. If the woman does not have the ability to get an abortion because it is banned, she may believe she is doomed to remain in that relationship.

Crystal Justice, chief external affairs officer for the National Domestic Violence Hotline, writes that because of abortion bans, abusive partners feel emboldened and justified in their use of reproductive coercion to control the survivor, which in many cases includes survivors being forced to become pregnant. . . . When you have laws that come along that are now stripping survivors of their bodily autonomy and right to control their own lives and health—which is exactly what abusive partners are trying to do—it is taking the harm even further.[39]

Men who use pregnancy to control women are using abortion bans as a tool to intensify their abuse. Women need access to abortion so that they can control their own reproduction and fight back from reproductive coercion. They also need access to abortion so they can avoid dangerous illegal abortions and dangerous situations in which they cannot get a lifesaving abortion.

Abortion Bans Are Not Harmful to Women

"I just reject the idea that as a woman I need abortion to be successful or to be as thriving as a man in my career. I don't think I need to sacrifice a life in order to do that."

—Phoebe Purvey, pro-life activist

Quoted in Ruth Graham, "'The Pro-life Generation': Young Women Fight Against Abortion Rights," *New York Times*, June 3, 2022. www.nytimes.com.

Consider these questions as you read:

1. In what ways do you think that abortion bans help or hurt women? Can you see some merits in the opposing arguments? Explain.
2. How much say should a parent have in whether their minor child gets an abortion or has a baby? Explain.
3. Other than abortion bans, what are some societal changes that might reduce the number of abortions?

Editor's note: The discussion that follows presents common arguments made in support of this perspective, reinforced by facts, quotes, and examples taken from various sources.

Abortion bans do not harm women, because they help prevent abortions—and abortions harm women. The pro-life position is about more than saving the lives of unborn children. It is about protecting women. Pro-choice arguments about the harm abortion bans allegedly inflict on women are based on claims that are inaccurate or oversimplified.

Exceptions for the Life of the Mother

One pro-choice argument against abortion bans is that they can stop a woman from getting an abortion that is necessary to save her life. This is simply untrue. According to the independent polling agency KFF, "All state abortion bans currently in effect contain exceptions to 'prevent the death' or 'preserve the life' of the pregnant person."[40] This includes states where abortion under all other circumstances has been banned.

Pro-choice advocates argue that abortion ban exceptions are too rigid. They claim that doctors are forced to postpone lifesaving abortions until a patient is actively dying. They point to the case of Amanda Zurawski, the Texas woman who almost died because doctors refused to give her a lifesaving abortion until it was almost too late.

However, according to Ingrid Skop, an obstetrician and gynecologist and abortion policy expert, the Zurawski case was a misapplication of Texas law. Texas law does allow a doctor to give a woman an emergency abortion if the physician knows the patient's life is likely to be in danger. "At the time of diagnosis of a potentially life-threatening pregnancy complication, physicians should be able to offer intervention," explains Skop, "and the current Texas law indicates that action is permissible."[41]

Abortion bans in places like Texas are only a few years old, and it is true that some states should revisit the wording of their laws to make sure women like Zurawski are not placed at risk. Fortunately, changes to these new abortion bans are happening. For example, in May 2023 the Oklahoma Supreme Court ruled that the state's abortion ban needed to be amended to make sure that doctors could perform abortions in cases like Amanda Zurawski's.

Abortion Coercion

Another pro-choice argument against abortion bans is that they enable reproductive coercion. According to this argument, men use pregnancy to force women to stay in abusive relationships, and the inability to get an abortion makes it harder for women to leave.

While situations like this exist, the argument overlooks how common another type of reproductive coercion is—abortion coercion. This is the use of pressure, intimidation, or force to coerce women into getting abortions they do not want. As reported in the online journal *Cureus*, a study of women in their forties who previously had abortions revealed that about 10 percent of them said their abortions had been coerced.

In her 2023 memoir, pop star Britney Spears wrote about her experience with abortion coercion. When she was seventeen, she got pregnant. Her boyfriend, pop star Justin Timberlake, pressured her into having an abortion. "Abortion was something I never could have imagined choosing for myself, but given the circumstances, this is what we did," she wrote. "If he didn't want to become a father, I didn't feel like I had much of a choice."[42]

The website Abort73 has hundreds of stories written by women who regret getting abortions, and many of these stories are about abortion coercion. An anonymous woman wrote:

> I found out I was pregnant at just three weeks and [my male partner] spent the next six weeks degrading me, intimidating me with talk of lawyers and lawsuits, breaking my heart, manipulating me, calling me names like "sleazy" and "disgusting," telling me I would be a horrible mother and never have the life I want, and promising me that he would not give child support but spend all of his money fighting for custody. I chose to have an abortion out of fear and emotional exhaustion.[43]

Sometimes abortion coercion comes from parents. On Abort73 an anonymous woman recounted how her parents demanded she get an abortion when she was seventeen. "Long-story-short is that my dad told me to either get an abortion or leave the house," she wrote. On the way to Planned Parenthood,

—Britney Spears, pop star

Women Are Harmed by Financial Insecurity, Not Abortion Bans

Public focus on the perceived harm of abortion bans distracts from a bigger problem for women: financial insecurity. According to a study published in 2023, 40 percent of women blame their abortions on being financially unprepared. In contrast, only 3 percent got an abortion because they did not want children. Unequal pay, low earnings, lack of paid maternal leave and health insurance all contribute to a lack of financial resources. These are the problems that harm women, not abortion bans.

Reason for Abortions	Percentage
Not financially prepared	40%
Not a good time	36%
Issues with a partner	31%
Need to focus on other children	29%
Interferes with future plans	20%
Not emotionally or mentally prepared	19%
Health issue	12%
Unable to provide a "good" life	12%
Not independent or mature enough	7%
Influence from family or friends	5%
Don't want children	3%

Source: Dawn Stacey, "Why Do People Have Abortions?," Verywell Health, August 7, 2023. www.verywellhealth.com.

her mother was infuriated by her tears. "My mom yelled at me and screamed at me and told me to just forget about it and forget that it ever happened and to never bring it up ever again,"[44] she said.

When a woman is coerced into having an abortion, she loses both her baby and her autonomy. Abortion bans take away the power of abusers to force women to have abortions.

Abortion Is a Superficial Solution to Larger Social Inequalities

Another pro-choice argument is that abortion bans harm women by forcing them to raise unplanned children without financial stability or community support. This is an oversimplification of a complex issue.

Many women do face daunting financial and personal challenges when faced with raising a child who was not planned. But abortion is not the solution. Abortion is the superficial solution to social problems that have negative consequences for all women. As Mary Szoch of the pro-life advocacy group Family Research Council argues, "No woman should have to abort her child to participate fully in society. If a pregnant woman or mother can't participate in society, the true feminist response is that something is wrong with society."[45]

In fact, studies show that many women choose abortion because of financial constraints—and not because they do not want children. According to the Turnaway Study, a comprehensive ten-year study on abortion, 40 percent of all women who choose to have abortions do so because they do not feel financially ready to have a baby. Another 12 percent feel they are not equipped to provide a good life for a baby. What this means is that many women in the United States are choosing abortions that they would not choose if they had more support in their lives.

The economic and social issues that make it challenging to have an unplanned child are many. Harmeet Kaur of CNN argues, "The US offers no national, paid parental leave program. Child care can be expensive or hard to find. And women are still more likely to shoulder the brunt of parenting responsibilities and household tasks."[46] Many young people are putting off having children because they are overwhelmed with student loan debt and the skyrocketing cost of housing. On top of that, women only make eighty-two cents for every dollar a man makes, and they often find themselves less respected in the workplace after having a child. And many college students who get pregnant feel like they have to choose between education and a baby, as few schools offer adequate resources to help young parents.

The organization Feminists for Life argues that abortion is not the solution to these problems. The solution is comprehensive societal changes that make it easier for a woman to raise an unplanned child—and to choose life. The organization's slogan is "Women deserve better than abortion," and its mission statement is "Feminists for Life of America recognizes that abortion is a reflection that our society has failed to meet the needs of women. We are dedicated to systematically eliminating the root causes that drive women to abortion—primarily lack of practical resources and support—through holistic, woman-centered solutions."[47]

Pro-choice advocates argue that abortion bans are harmful to women. But the opposite is true. They prevent abortion from being used as a superficial solution to structural problems that harm all women. Abortion bans also protect women against abortion coercion and include exceptions to allow abortions in life-threatening situations.

> "Abortion is a reflection that our society has failed to meet the needs of women."[47]
>
> —Feminists for Life of America mission statement

Source Notes

Overview: Abortion Rights

1. Quoted in Caroline Kitchener, "This Texas Teen Wanted an Abortion. She Now Has Twins," *Washington Post*, June 22, 2022. www.washingtonpost.com.
2. Zara Abrams, "Abortion Bans Cause Outsized Harm for People of Color," American Psychological Association, June 1, 2023. www.apa.org.
3. Quoted in National Women's Law Center, "*Roe v. Wade* and the Right to an Abortion," 2024. https://nwlc.org.

Chapter One: Should Women Have the Legal Right to Choose Abortion?

4. United Nations Population Fund, "What Is Bodily Autonomy?," 2021. www.unfpa.org.
5. Natalia Kanem, "Human Rights Require Bodily Autonomy for All—at All Times: Statement by UNFPA Executive Director on Human Rights Day," United Nations Population Fund, December 9, 2023. www.unfpa.org.
6. Kathryn Kolbert and Julie F. Kay, *Controlling Women: What We Must Do Now to Save Reproductive Freedom*. New York: Hachette, 2021, p. 16.
7. Quoted in Brennan Center for Justice, "*Roe v. Wade* and Supreme Court Abortion Cases," September 28, 2022. www.brennancenter.org.
8. Cindy Hyde-Smith campaign website, "Defending Life and Protecting the Unborn." www.cindyhydesmith.com.
9. US Constitution, Amendment I.
10. University of Illinois Chicago Women's Leadership and Resource Center, "Reproductive Oppression Against Black Women," 2023. https://wlrc.uic.edu.
11. National Women's Law Center, "Abortion Rights and Access Are Inextricably Tied to Equality and Gender Justice," August 10, 2022. www.nwlc.org.
12. Quoted in Charlie Camosy, "'Unimaginable Cruelty and Trauma'": A Survivor of Forced Sterilization Speaks Out," Pillar, August 19, 2022. www.pillarcatholic.com.

13. Heritage Foundation, "Why Should Government Protect Life?," 2024. www.heritage.org.
14. Cleveland Clinic, "Fetal Development," March 3, 2023. http://my .clevelandclinic.org.
15. Danielle Pitzer, "When Does a Fetus Become a Baby?," Focus on the Family, August 31, 2023. www.focuonthefamily.com.
16. Live Action, "When Does Life Begin?," 2023. www.liveaction.org.
17. Abort73, "Part of the Mother's Body?," August 12, 2019. www .abort73.com.
18. United Nations, Universal Declaration of Human Rights, Article 7, December 10, 1948. www.un.org.
19. Abort73, "Competing Rights," August 14, 2019. www.abort73.com.

Chapter Two: Should Medication Abortion Be Easily Accessible?

20. Amy Shoenfeld Walker et al., "Are Abortion Pills Safe? Here's the Evidence," *New York Times*, April 7, 2023. www.nytimes.com.
21. Annette Choi and Will Mullery, "How Safe Is the Abortion Pill Compared with Other Common Drugs?," CNN Health, December 13, 2023. www.cnn.com.
22. Quoted in Beth Mole, "The Supreme Court Battle over the Abortion Pill and FDA Authority, Explained [Updated]," Ars Technica, April 19, 2023. https://arstechnica.com.
23. American Civil Liberties Union, "What Is Mifepristone and Why Is It Essential to Abortion Access?," February 2, 2023. www.aclu.com.
24. Quoted in Claire Cain Miller and Margot Sanger-Katz, "Medication Abortions Are Increasing: What They Are and Where Women Get Them," *New York Times*, May 9, 2022. www.nytimes.com.
25. Quoted in Christen A. Johnson, "'It Was Really Empowering'—5 Women Reflect on Their Medication Abortion Experience," *Cosmopolitan*, May 10, 2023. www.cosmopolitan.com.
26. Quoted in Johnson, "'It Was Really Empowering.'"
27. Quoted in Johnson, "'It Was Really Empowering.'"
28. Quoted in Danielle Campoamor, "39 Abortion Stories Show Just How Important Abortion Access Is," *Teen Vogue*, January 9, 2020. www.teenvogue.com.
29. Walker et al., "Are Abortion Pills Safe?"
30. Alyssa Billingsley, "9 Abortion Pill (Mifepristone and Misoprostol) Side Effects and How to Manage Them," GoodRx Health, March 24, 2023. www.goodrx.com.
31. Quoted in Shefali Luthra, "Medication Abortion Is the Nation's Future. What Does It Feel Like?," The 19th, May 23, 2022. https://19news .com.

32. Quoted in Rachel Rasker, "What Taking Medication Abortion Pills Was like for Jessica," ABC Everyday, May 11, 2022. www.abc.net.au.

33. Quoted in Ruth Reader, "The Web Is Home to an Illegal Bazaar for Abortion Pills. The FDA Is Ill-Equipped to Stop It," Politico, August 1, 2022. www.politico.com.

34. Quoted in Maria Lencki, "Women Are Turning to the Black Market to Get 'Dangerous' Abortion Pills, Pro-life Organization Says," Fox News, December 2, 2023. www.foxnews.com.

Chapter Three: Are Abortion Bans Harmful to Women?

35. Phyllis, "I Had an Illegal Abortion Before *Roe v. Wade*," Planned Parenthood, March 15, 2022. www.plannedparenthood.org.

36. Quoted in Michaeleen Doucleff, "Do Restrictive Abortion Laws Actually Reduce Abortion? A Global Map Offers Insights," National Public Radio, June 27, 2022. www.npr.org.

37. Brittni Frederiksen et al., "A National Survey of OBGYNs' Experiences After *Dobbs*," KFF, June 21, 2023. www.kff.org.

38. Quoted in Elizabeth Cohen and John Bonified, "Texas Woman Almost Dies Because She Couldn't Get An Abortion," CNN, June 20, 2023. www.cnn.com.

39. Quoted in Carter Sherman, "Domestic Abusers Are Using Abortion Bans to Control Their Victims," *Vice*, July 13, 2023. www.vice.com.

40. Mabel Felix et al., "A Review of Exceptions in State Abortion Bans: Implications for the Provision of Abortion Services," KFF, May 18, 2023. www.kff.org.

41. Ingrid Skop, "Abortion Policy Allows Physicians to Intervene to Protect a Mother's Life," Charlotte Lozier Institute, May 16, 2023. www.lozierinstitute.org.

42. Quoted in Zoe Guy, "Justin Timberlake 'Thought Maybe Music Would Help' Britney Spears's Abortion," *Vulture*, October 23, 2023. www.vulture.com.

43. Anonymous. "Abortion Story," Abort73, December 1, 2023. www.abort73.com.

44. Anonymous, "Abortion Story: Albany, NY," Abort73, June 27, 2021. www.abort73.com.

45. Mary Szoch, ed., *The Best Pro-life Arguments for Secular Audiences*. Washington, DC: Center for Human Dignity at Family Research Council, 2021, p. 19.

46. Harmeet Kaur, "Why More Women Are Choosing Not to Have Kids," CNN, September 25, 2023. www.cnn.com.

47. Feminists for Life of America, "About Us," 2020. www.feministsforlife.org.

Abortion Rights Facts

Public Opinion About Abortion

- According to a May 2023 Gallup poll, 34 percent of Americans believe abortion should be legal under any circumstances, 51 percent believe it should be legal under certain circumstances, and 13 percent believe it should be illegal in all circumstances.
- The Gallup poll also shows that 63 percent of Americans believe mifepristone (the primary drug used in medication abortions) should be available as a prescription drug.
- According to the Pew Research Center, 74 percent of Americans under age thirty think abortion should be legal in all or most cases.
- The Pew Research Center also found that 57 percent of Americans disapprove of the *Dobbs* decision that overturned *Roe v. Wade*.
- According to a 2022 University of Pennsylvania poll, 94 percent of Democrats and 76 percent of Republicans believe a woman should be able to get an abortion in cases of rape or incest.

Abortion Demographics

- According to KFF, about 70 percent of abortion patients are women of color.
- The *New York Times* reports that about half of women who get abortions have incomes below the poverty level.
- The *New York Times* also reports that about 60 percent of women who have abortions have previously given birth.
- According to the Pew Research Center, about 87 percent of women who have abortions are unmarried.
- According to the Guttmacher Institute, about 16 percent of people getting abortions identify as LGBTQ.

Abortion After the 2022 *Dobbs v. Jackson Women's Health Organization* Supreme Court Decision

- *PBS NewsHour* reports that as of June 2023, 25 million women live in states where abortion is illegal in many or most cases.
- According to the Society of Family Planning, there were twenty-two hundred more legal abortions in the United States from July 2022 to June 2023 than in the previous year.
- CNN reports that in the first half of 2023, there were thirty-two thousand more births than expected in states with abortion bans.
- CNN also reports that in the year after the *Dobbs* decision, the number of medication abortions via telehealth increased by 136 percent.
- According to the Guttmacher Institute, the number of pregnant women traveling to another state to have an abortion has increased from one in ten in 2020 to one in five in 2023.

Abort73

www.abort73.com

A project of Loxafamosity Ministries, Abort73 is a Christian website that includes detailed arguments in support of pro-life positions, along with statistics and resources. It also includes hundreds of anonymous stories purportedly written by women who regret having abortions.

Feminists for Life of America

www.feministsforlife.com

This pro-life organization advocates for societal changes so that women have more resources and support when choosing to have children. Its website includes feminist answers to pro-life questions as well as resources for teens as part of its Girls Deserve Better program. The site also includes information about how many women's rights advocates have historically opposed abortion.

Focus on the Family

www.focusonthefamily.com

Focus on the Family is an evangelical Christian organization that advocates for socially conservative political positions with a strong emphasis on promoting pro-life legislation and views. Its website includes many videos that explain pro-life positions, as well as resources for women who are considering abortion.

Guttmacher Institute

www.guttmacher.org

This research organization conducts studies related to reproductive issues, including abortion. It advocates for policy changes worldwide that give women greater reproductive autonomy. Its website contains information about how many abortions are done each year, as well as information about US abortion policy.

Planned Parenthood

www.plannedparenthood.org

Planned Parenthood is an organization that operates reproductive health care clinics. These services include gynecological exams, birth control prescriptions, and abortions (in states where this is legal). It is also an advocacy group, and its website has extensive information about abortion, contraception, pregnancy, sexual violence, and other women's health issues.

Religious Coalition for Reproductive Choice

https://rcrc.org

The Religious Coalition for Reproductive Choice is an interfaith organization that promotes pro-choice arguments rooted in diverse religious beliefs. Its website features free or twenty-five-dollar short courses, exploring how pro-choice perspectives align with various faith traditions.

Reproductive Freedom for All

www.reproductivefreedomforall.org

Formerly known as NARAL Pro-Choice America, Reproductive Freedom for All is a pro-choice advocacy group that is currently focused on fighting for the restoration of abortion rights in states where abortion is restricted or banned. Its website includes information about ways to get involved with pro-choice activism.

Susan B. Anthony Pro-Life America

https://sbaprolife.org

This organization focuses on promoting pro-life political candidates. It provides a Pro-Life Scorecard that grades politicians based on the degree to which they support pro-life legislation. Its website includes pro-life resources for pregnant women.

For Further Research

Books

Becca Andrews, *No Choice: The Destruction of* Roe v. Wade *and the Fight to Protect a Fundamental American Right*. New York: Hachette, 2022.

Steven A. Christie, *Speaking for the Unborn: 30-Second Pro-life Rebuttals to Pro-choice Arguments*. Steubensville, OH: Emmaus Road, 2022.

Patti Giebnick. *Unexpected Choice: An Abortion Doctor's Journey to Pro-life*. Carol Springs, IL: Tyndale House, 2021.

Kathryn Kolbert and Julie F. Kay, *Controlling Women: What We Must Do Now to Save Reproductive Freedom*. New York: Hachette, 2021.

Felicia Kornbluh, *A Woman's Life Is a Human Life: My Mother, Our Neighbor, and the Journey from Reproductive Rights to Reproductive Justice*. New York: Grove, 2023.

Lila Rose, *Fighting for Life: Becoming a Force for Change in a Wounded World*. Nashville, TN: Nelson, 2022.

Benjamin Watson, *The New Fight for Life:* Roe*, Race, and a Pro-life Commitment to Justice*. Carol Springs, IL: Tyndale Momentum, 2023.

Mary Ziegler, Roe*: The History of a National Obsession*. New Haven, CT: Yale University Press, 2023.

Internet Sources

Rhyma Castillo, "Here's Why the Abortion Debate Is Even More Complex than You Ever Thought," Elite Daily, July 21, 2021. www.elitedaily.com.

Annette Choi and Will Mullery, "How Safe Is the Abortion Pill Compared with Other Common Drugs?," CNN Health, December 13, 2023. www.cnn.com.

Ross Douthat, "The Case Against Abortion," *New York Times*, November 30, 2021. www.nytimes.com.

Gallup, "Where Do Americans Stand on Abortion?," July 7, 2023. https://news.gallup.com.

Ruth Graham, "'The Pro-life Generation': Young Women Fight Against Abortion Rights," *New York Times*, June 3, 2022. www.nytimes.com.

Ed Kilgore, "Everything You Need to Know About the Abortion Debate," *New York*, May 5, 2022. www.nymag.com.

Pew Research Center, "America's Abortion Quandary," May 6, 2022. www.pewresearch.org.

Melissa Quinn, "A Timeline of the Abortion Debate at the Supreme Court, from *Roe v. Wade* to Its End," CBS News, June 26, 2022. www.cbsnews.com.

Mary Szoch, ed., "The Best Pro-life Arguments for Secular Audiences," Center for Human Dignity at Family Research Council, 2021. www.frc.org.

Amy Shoenfeld Walker et al., "Are Abortion Pills Safe? Here's the Evidence," *New York Times*, April 7, 2023. www.nytimes.com.

About the Author

Naomi Rockler is an author of nonfiction and fiction books for kids, an educational writer, and a former professor and instructional designer. She lives in Minneapolis with her husband, daughter, two cats, and a dog.